Praise for Storyshares

"One of the brightest innovators and game-changers in the education industry."
— Forbes

"Your success in applying research-validated practices to promote literacy serves as a valuable model for other organizations seeking to create evidence-based literacy programs."
— Library of Congress

"We need powerful social and educational innovation, and Storyshares is breaking new ground. The organization addresses critical problems facing our students and teachers. I am excited about the strategies it brings to the collective work of making sure every student has an equal chance in life."
— Teach For America

"It's the perfect idea. There's really nothing like this. I mean, wow, this will be a wonderful experience for young people."
— Andrea Davis Pinkney, Executive Director, Scholastic

"Reading for meaning opens opportunities for a lifetime of learning. Providing emerging readers with engaging texts that are designed to offer both challenges and support for each individual will improve their lives for years to come. Storyshares is a wonderful start."
— David Rose, Co-founder of CAST & UDL

Storyshares presents

Published by Storyshares, LLC

Storyshares
Storyshares, LLC
24 N. Bryn Mawr Avenue #340
Bryn Mawr, Pennsylvania 19010-3304
www.storyshares.org

Inspiring reading with a new kind of book.

Interest Level: High School
Grade Level Equivalent: 2.2

ISBN 9781642611366
Book design by Saskia Globig

BLUE SNOW

Kevin James Moore

Storyshares

CONTENTS

CHAPTER ONE

My dad said I had to try harder in school. I sat in the car with my parents, getting ready to go back.

"Paul, study more. We love you," said Mom. She gave me a little kiss on my cheek.

"If you need anything, call us," said Dad. He shook my hand and patted my shoulder.

I grabbed my blue suitcase and my backpack. Opened the car door. I got out, and my parents drove away.

The air was cold. Small snowflakes were blowing in the wind. I wiped my cheek to make sure Mom hadn't left any red lipstick. I didn't want the other boys to make fun of me. I don't like being laughed at.

I walked toward the giant stone building of Willow Hill Academy. There was snow on the roof and on top of all the tree branches. It looked like someone dripped white paint over everything.

My boots crunched the snow under my feet. Steam came out of my mouth as I exhaled the cold air. The first half of freshman year had been harder than I had imagined. The only class I'd gotten an A in was Art. I thought back to when my parents saw my report card over Christmas vacation. They'd had a talk with me about school. They weren't happy with my grades.

"Sit down on the couch, Paul," Dad had said.

"We aren't mad at you," my mom had added, with a sweet smile on her face.

I'd seen the letter from Willow Hill Academy in my dad's hands.

Mom had sat next to my dad, holding his arm. I'd been nervous. Drops of sweat had formed on the back of my neck. I always sweat first behind my ears.

My dad then removed his glasses from his face. He'd gently placed his glasses on the table next to him.

"Paul, you can do better than this," he'd said. "C in Math, C in History, D in English. What's going on at school?"

"I can't read as fast as the other kids. The only class I like is Art," I'd said. "The only time I can sit still and focus is when I'm drawing or painting. I always imagine things I want to paint when I'm sitting in those other classes."

"You are a great artist, Paul. But you have to do well in your other classes, too," my mom had told me.

I'd promised them I would.

I was going to do better in school.

But the only thing I'd been able to think about after talking to my parents was an elf throwing a snowball at Santa. So I'd gone upstairs to my room and opened my notebook to draw a picture of a snowball exploding against Santa's big belly.

Chapter Two

I pulled on the big, red, heavy, wooden door of the school and walked in. Inside was warm. All the boys were laughing and yelling. They were throwing paper airplanes at each other.

I heard someone yell my name.

"Paul Joyce!" It was Thunder Jenkins. His real name was Greg. Everyone called him Thunder, though, because he could burp louder than anyone at school.

He yelled my name again. I started walking towards him, stopping for a second when a paper airplane soared in front of my face.

Thunder was leaning against the stone wall of the

hallway. The light above him illuminated the top of his head. It made his blond hair look like it was made out of gold and fire. Next to him stood Scott Fitzgerald. Scott was thin and his clothes always seemed too big for him.

They were both waving me over. Thunder and Scott were my best friends.

"How was Christmas?" asked Thunder.

"It was okay, but my parents saw my report card," I said.

"Bummer," said Scott. "Were they mad at you?"

I shrugged my shoulders. I didn't feel like talking about it. "Not really. They told me to try harder," I said.

"Are you going to the dance tonight?" Scott asked.

"Yeah. You can't miss those Ashby Prep girls," said Thunder.

"I don't know," I said.

That night was the Winter Dance with the all-girls school, Ashby Prep. It was the only time all year that the two schools mingle. The boys' school and the girls' school never saw each other, otherwise. The rest of the year, a giant, twenty-foot brick wall separated Willow Hill Academy from Ashby Prep.

All of the boys were excited to go. Except me. I wanted to spend the night in my room. I was feeling down about my grades. I wasn't in the mood for dancing.

Scott, Thunder, and I stopped talking and went upstairs to our dorms. I shared a room with Scott, and Thunder lived three doors down the hall with Matt Crane.

Matt Crane was the smelliest boy in the entire school. He had a weird, mixed odor of sweaty socks and sardines. I really believed Thunder couldn't smell Matt. Thunder was the only boy that didn't seem to mind the smell. He and Matt got along very well and were good friends. And since Matt was Thunder's friend, he was Scott's friend, and mine too.

I began to unpack my suitcase when I got into my room. I put my clothes into the dresser and hung my coats in the closet. Then I walked over and flopped backwards onto my bed. It felt like floating on top of the ocean. I laid with my hands resting on my chest and I closed my eyes.

"Don't fall asleep, Paul," said Scott. "You have to go to the dance. You can't miss our first chance to meet Ashby girls."

"I'm only resting for a minute," I said.

"Get up and help me put my suitcase on the top shelf in the closet. I'm too short," said Scott.

I walked over to the closet and stood on my tiptoes to put away Scott's suitcase.

"Thanks," Scott said. "Now, let's get ready for the dance."

I sat back down on my bed. "I'm not sure I want to go," I said.

Scott wouldn't take no for an answer. "Get up and put on a suit and tie. You don't even have to dance. If you don't go, you'll regret it tomorrow," he said.

Thunder burst into our room and flung the door open.

"You guys ready? Paul, why are you sitting on your bed? You have to come."

"Okay, fine. I can't sit still any longer, anyway. Plus, I have to see you in public dressed like that, Thunder," I said.

"What's wrong with what I'm wearing?" he asked.

Scott and I looked at each other and laughed. "You look like a marshmallow, dude," Scott told Thunder.

"What are you talking about? I look good," replied Thunder.

Thunder was dressed all in white. Everything from head to toe.

He even had on white socks. The only thing on him that wasn't white were the black buttons going down his shirt. They looked like round, shiny beetles marching single file down his chest.

"The girls are going to love it," Thunder said, before letting out a roaring burp.

"That's gross," said Scott.

Scott and I got ready for the dance. I put on a black jacket and a blue shirt. I checked the mirror to make sure I got my tie right, then took an extra moment to examine my face.

I carefully studied my eyes, my mouth, my hair. My hair was always messy. To me it looked like my hair was swirled onto my head by a frozen yogurt machine. But this was the best I was going to get myself to look.

As Scott, Thunder, and I walked down the hall, Matt ran up to us. The four of us started walking toward Ashby Prep.

Chapter Three

The air was chilly, so we walked close to each other to stay warm. A group of senior boys were in front of us. They were hooting and hollering. Making lots of loud noise and jumping around. Seeing the senior boys have so much fun made us all more excited. I started to think that I really could have a good time at the dance.

At closer distance, Ashby Prep looked a lot different from our school. It was made of wood instead of stone and bricks. The girls' school looked like a large and elaborate cabin. To me it resembled the castle of an old Viking king.

We knocked the snow from our shoes as we entered. The inside was magnificent. It was beautifully decorated for the dance. There were large paper snowflakes hung all over the halls and in the atrium. There were also shiny blue and silver ribbons, and matching blue and silver balloons.

The atrium was a large and spacious room with a glass ceiling on which patches of snow had settled. Tables were placed near the wall to create a dance floor in the middle. Pale blue light from the full moon shone through the ceiling, and made tiny spotlights all over the dance floor.

"Let's go talk to the girls!" exclaimed Thunder.

"I'm going to get some soda first," I said.

Scott and Matt agreed with me, and Thunder thought drinking some soda first wasn't a bad idea. I was very nervous. There were so many kids. So many girls. Some people were already dancing. I didn't know what to do. I didn't even know where to stand.

The four of us stood together with our sodas, checking out the room. Everyone seemed to be having fun.

"Okay, boys, time to find a girl to dance with," said Thunder. He went off with Scott and Matt and headed toward a group of girls. The girls were standing side by side and talking.

Thunder and Scott joined in on their conversation. I couldn't tell what they were saying, but I saw the girls start to laugh.

Next, they were all out on the floor dancing with each other.

20

I was watching them, and drinking my soda when a soft voice spoke to me.

"Looks like fun. Why aren't you dancing with your friends?"

I turned and saw the most beautiful girl I had ever seen.

She had soft, flowing brown hair down to her shoulders. Her eyes matched the blue balloons that floated all over the room. She wore a pale dress that mimicked the color of the moon.

"I'm drinking soda. Mixing soda with my dancing could be hazardous," I said.

"Your dancing can't be that bad. I'm sure that soda won't fizz up and explode," she laughed. "My name is Anna Gambler. What's yours?"

"I'm... I'm Paul Joyce," I said.

"Well, Paul Joyce, do you want to dance?" Anna asked.

I was trying to say "yes," but my tongue was tied in knots. I started to feel sweat behind my left ear. I was too shocked and nervous to speak. Anna grabbed my hand. I put my soda down on the table. Anna dragged me to the dance floor.

"I can't dance," I warned.

"No one here is a great dancer. It's about having fun," said Anna.

At first, I barely moved. I swayed slowly, side to side. I felt like a flag moving in a soft wind.

"Paul, you have to move. Don't worry what everyone else will think," said Anna.

So I moved my hands up and down. Anna laughed a little. I felt awkward. I wasn't used to moving so many different parts of my body. I didn't know how to move my hands and feet at the same time. I also had to move them in different directions.

"Good job. Now move your feet like this," Anna said. She was twisting her feet and moving her shoulders.

I tried my best to imitate her. I copied everything she was doing.

"You're a liar, Paul," Anna joked. "You're a terrific dancer."

I smiled.

"Yeah, this isn't so bad," I said.

Then the song stopped. A slow song came on. I stood still, and looked at Anna. I had no clue what to do. I had just learned to dance to a fast song. I didn't know how to dance to a slow one.

Anna moved closer to me. She held my left hand up near our shoulders. She then placed my other hand on the bottom of her back.

"Don't be so nervous, Paul. I'll teach you what to do."

"Okay," I said.

I could feel my hands get a little moist. I was beginning to sweat more. Hopefully, Anna didn't think it was gross.

We started to glide around the dance floor.

Chapter Four

I forgot about everyone as I danced with Anna. All I saw was her. All I could hear was the music. I felt as if Anna and I were all alone, and dancing in our own world. It was terrific.

"I want you to dip me," Anna said.

"I'm not sure I know how," I said.

"I'm going to lean back. Put your hand on my back and make sure I don't fall," Anna instructed.

I did exactly what Anna told me. When she leaned backwards her head tilted back. When she bent her head back, her brown hair cascaded down and almost touched the floor. Her hair looked like a waterfall of milk chocolate.

She popped back up and gazed at me. Anna was smiling and giggling with delight. "That was wonderful, Paul. I'm having such a fantastic time," Anna said.

"I'm having a great time, too. I'm not nervous anymore. Let me try to twirl you," I said.

Anna nodded her head and said "Okay."

I lifted my hand up high and turned my wrist, and Anna began to twirl. She spun on her toes. Her hair and the bottom of her dress spun with her.

Anna was twirling when the music stopped. I didn't know how to stop her. She got through another spin and then fell on her butt. I thought she was going to be mad at me, but Anna sat on the floor laughing.

"That was so much fun," she said.

I laughed, too.

"Are you all right, Anna?" I asked.

"Yes. I'm perfect," she said.

We decided to go outside to cool off, and to get some fresh air. Anna went to grab her coat, and then we went outside.

Snow was still falling. The moonlight shining on all the snow made it seem like everything was glowing blue.

"That was a lot of fun," Anna said. A small trail of steam escaped from her mouth and followed every word.

"I can't believe I actually danced," I said.

"I told you that you had nothing to worry about," she said.

"I was nervous at the beginning, but I was having a blast by the end. I can't believe you fell on your butt," I said.

"I know. We'll have to work on that for next time."

"Next time?" I asked, surprised.

"Of course, Paul. I'm not going to disappear. I like you," Anna said with a big smile.

I held her hands and smiled back.

Anna hugged me and gave me a kiss on my cheek. I felt my face warm up.

"Paul, your face is all red," Anna said.

I was blushing, but I didn't want to admit it. I was a little embarrassed.

"It must be the cold weather," I lied.

Anna laughed. "You are so silly and fun," she said. "Wow, it's getting late. I have to go."

"Wait, Anna. How do I talk to you?" I asked.

"Do you know where the ivy is on the wall between the two schools?" Anna asked.

"Yes," I replied.

"On the far right side, actually, the far *left* on your side of the wall, there is a brick missing. You can leave letters for me there. I'll leave letters for you there too. We can check it every day and write to each other," she said.

"That's fantastic," I said.

We smiled at each other. Then Anna checked her watch.

"It's late. I really have to go now, Paul," she said.

"Okay," I said.

Anna told me she had a wonderful time. She said goodbye and began walking away. I watched her as she began to vanish into the falling snow. Then Anna stopped and turned back to me.

"Don't forget to check the wall," she yelled.

"I won't, Anna," I yelled back, waving goodbye.

Chapter Five

I was almost back at my dorm. I had thought about Anna the entire time I was walking. Then I slapped my hand against my forehead. I had completely forgotten about my friends.

I had such a terrific time with Anna that I forgot about everything else.

It was too late to go back and find them. I decided to go back to my room and wait. Scott, Thunder, and Matt would have to be back soon.

Scott and Thunder burst through the door laughing. I was laying on my bed thinking about dancing with Anna.

"Where did you go, Paul?" asked Thunder.

"I came back a little early," I said.

"We had a terrific time dancing with all of those Ashby girls. You should've been with us, Paul," Scott said.

"I had a great time too," I told Thunder and Scott.

"Yeah, we saw you dancing. What was the girl's name?" asked Scott.

"Her name was Anna, and she's amazing," I said.

"All those Ashby girls are amazing. Too bad we don't get to see them again," Thunder said.

Thunder was right. I wouldn't see Anna again for a long time. We could only write to each other.

"Okay, guys, I'm going to bed. Matt is already in bed, probably. I'll see you in school," Thunder said. Then he left and closed the door.

"Tonight was the best. Thunder was ridiculous in his white suit. Even Matt had girls dancing with him. I guess he didn't smell too bad," Scott said, laughing.

I didn't say anything back. I stared at the ceiling wondering if I'd ever see Anna again.

"Paul. Earth to Paul. What's wrong?" asked Scott.

"I have to see Anna again," I said.

"Relax. You can see her during the summer after school ends," said Scott.

"I don't know if I can wait that long," I told Scott.

"Maybe you'll figure something out. We have to go to bed now, because we have school tomorrow. Go to sleep and we'll think of something this week," said Scott.

Scott turned off the lights.

I thought of Anna until I fell asleep.

Chapter Six

Mr. Clutterbuck asked me to stay after English. He wanted to talk to me, because he saw me daydreaming. On top of reading *The Great Gatsby*, Mr. Clutterbuck gave me a book on Leonardo da Vinci. He told me it was for extra credit.

I was thinking about what I should write to Anna in my letter. I wanted to write an amazing letter, but I couldn't think of anything brilliant.

Finally, I wrote what I was thinking. I told Anna how amazing it was to meet her, and how much fun I had at the dance.

After my last class, I ran to the wall with my letter. The wall was covered with snow. Snow also sat on top of the green leaves of the ivy.

I remembered what Anna had said and I went to the edge of the ivy on the wall. I looked, but didn't see a brick missing. My hand pushed the ivy to the side, and I saw the hole in the wall.

Anna already had a letter waiting for me. I put my letter in the wall and took Anna's letter out. I couldn't wait to read it. I opened her letter immediately.

Anna wrote that she'd had a wonderful time dancing. She said that meeting me was the best thing about the dance. She had thought about me all night, she wrote.

I felt my face get warm again after reading Anna's letter. It was the same feeling I got when she had kissed me on the cheek.

For the next month Anna and I exchanged letters. Every day after my last class I went to the wall to find a letter waiting for me.

Anna left me a photo of herself in one of her letters. Looking at her photo was the only way I could see her.

I would draw her face in my sketchbook. I drew her doing all kinds of activities that she would write about. I drew pictures of her ice skating, reading, and making snow angels.

Sometimes, I would put my drawings of her in my letters.

It was exciting to get her letters and to write her back. Every time I read her letters I would blush. My cheeks would turn red.

At night I would do my homework as fast as I could. This gave me more time to read Anna's letters again.

Since I was doing my homework my grades improved. I had a B in almost all my classes. English was the only class I still had a C in.

Chapter Seven

I had received a B+ on my paper about *The Great Gatsby*. Mr. Clutterbuck asked me to stay after class again to talk. "Paul, excellent job on your paper. Your writing has improved recently," Mr. Clutterbuck said.

"Thanks. I really focused on my work this time. I liked this book. It made it easier to read," I said.

"Have you come up with an extra credit project on da Vinci yet?" asked Mr. Clutterbuck.

"I'm still thinking of something," I told him.

"Good. I know you're good at art, Paul. Try to do something like da Vinci," he said.

"I'm going to. Bye," I said.

"See you next class," he said.

As I walked between classes, I began to think of da Vinci's ornithopter. It was a flying machine he designed as a pair of wings to make a man fly like a bird.

It occurred to me that if I could build an ornithopter, I could fly over the wall. Then I would be able to see Anna.

To build the wings I was going to need help from my friends.

That night in my dorm room, Scott, Thunder, and Matt came for a secret meeting. I told them I was going to build a pair of wings like a bird. Then I would fly over the wall to Ashby to see Anna.

"This sounds crazy," said Matt.

"It sounds awesome to me," said Thunder.

"I'm going to need help from you guys," I told them.

"Whatever you need. We're here to help," Scott said.

"Great! We need some wood to build a frame and some bed sheets. Also some nails, glue, and belts. It only has to fly thirty-three feet. I have to fly from the top of Goat Hill to the other side of the wall," I said.

"Let's get going, guys," said Thunder. He let out a loud burp and walked out of the room.

"Okay. You heard Thunder. Let's get to work," I said. I was filled with excitement.

My friends and I gathered all the materials to build the wings. Over the next few days, we started to assemble them. We built the wood frame first.

I wrote to Anna and told her about my plan. She thought it was crazy. I assured her the wings were going to work.

I was going to fly over the wall to see her.

Chapter Eight

By the fourth day, the wings were almost done. Each wing was six feet long and would strap to my arms with belts. All that was left was to attach the bedsheets.

"Guys, we have to make sure that the sheets are stretched as tightly as possible over the wood," I instructed.

"We've got it, Paul," Scott said.

Thunder and Matt glued and stapled the sheet to the front of the wing. Then Scott and I pulled the sheet over the wing as tight as we could. As we held the sheet tight, Thunder and Matt stapled and glued the rest of the sheet to the wing.

We then did the exact same thing to the other wing.

"These look awesome," said Thunder.

I stood there smiling. I couldn't believe we had done it. I had made wings to fly to Anna.

"Try them on," Scott said.

I strapped the wing to my right arm and flapped it up and down like a bird. "It feels great. I can feel the wing catching the air," I said.

"Are you going to test them out?" Scott asked.

"There's not enough time. Tomorrow I'll have to fly," I said.

I wrote a letter to Anna. I told her the wings were finished and that tomorrow after school I was coming to see her.

I ran to the wall and left the letter.

It was hard to sleep that night, because I was so excited.

I woke up in the morning and gazed at the wings. They were marvelous and cool.

School went by so slowly that day. All I wanted to do was fly, but the clock seemed to be taking longer than ever to reach 4 p.m.

Finally, school ended and my friends and I raced to my room. Thunder and Matt grabbed one wing. Scott and I grabbed the other. We started running toward Goat Hill.

As we ran, all the other students stopped and stared at us carrying the wings. We ran by Mr. Clutterbuck and I heard him shout, "Paul, what are you doing?"

"Extra credit!" I shouted back.

We finally made it to the top of Goat Hill. My friends helped me strap on the wings. I moved my arms. The wings felt good.

"Are you ready?" Scott asked.

"Yes. All I have to do is fly thirty-three feet," I said.

At the bottom of the hill, a bunch of the other students had gathered. They were curious. They wanted to see what I was doing.

Mr. Clutterbuck started walking up the hill. He was telling me to stop. He said if I didn't stop that I would have detention for a month. It was too late. I was ready to fly.

"It's now or never. Time for takeoff," Thunder said.

I took a few steps backwards. Then I started to run as fast as I could. When I got to the top of the hill, I jumped.

Chapter Nine

I was flying. I was soaring like a bird.

The wind rushed past me and filled my wings with air. I flapped my arms and I went a little higher.

I could see over the wall. I could see Anna.

Right before I reached the wall, a part of the sheet on the left wing came loose. I started to fall. I flapped my wings as hard as I could.

I felt my feet hit the top of the wall. I fell and tumbled onto the ground. My face was buried in snow.

Someone came over and helped me up. I wiped the snow from my face and opened my eyes.

It was Anna and she was smiling at me.

I had done it. I had flown over the wall. Well, not all the way over. I had only flown thirty-two and a half feet, but it was enough to make it.

"Paul, you're crazy. I can't believe you did that," Anna said.

"I told you I was going to fly to you. I had to see you again, Anna," I said.

"You looked magnificent flying through the air," she told me.

Anna then gave me a big hug. "Now promise me you'll walk to me next time," she said.

"I will," I told her.

I stood up and took off the wings. Anna hugged me again. I was so excited to see her brown hair, her blue eyes, and big smile.

Then, without thinking, I kissed her.

I was still kissing her when I felt someone pull us apart. It was Mr. Clutterbuck. He had walked over to Ashby.

"Stop it, you two. Paul, are you okay?" he asked.

"Yeah. I feel great," I replied.

"Good, because you have detention for a month," Mr. Clutterbuck said. "Now let's go back."

I hugged Anna again, and she kissed me.

"Write to me, Paul," she said.

"I promise, Anna," I said.

I waved bye as Mr. Clutterbuck pulled me away.

"Was all of that worth it, Paul?" he asked.

"You tell me. Did I get the extra credit?" I said. I was still blushing from kissing Anna.

About the Author

Kevin James Moore wrote *Blue Snow* for the first Storyshares contest. He says, "It seemed like a great way to write a neat story and help people get into reading. I want to write enjoyable stories. I also want people to read. As I've gotten older, I've noticed there are less people I know that read. I like talking about books and authors but there's no one around."

"So," he implores, "please read so I have someone to talk with!"

About the Publisher

Storyshares is a publisher focused on supporting the millions of teens and adults who struggle with reading by creating a new shelf in the library specifically for them. The ever-growing collection features content that is compelling and culturally relevant for teens and adults, yet still readable at a range of lower reading levels.

Storyshares generates content by engaging deeply with writers, bringing together a community to create this new kind of book. With more intriguing and approachable stories to choose from, the teens and adults who have fallen behind are improving their skills and beginning to discover the joy of reading.

For more information, visit storyshares.org.

Easy to Read. Hard to Put Down.

www.ingramcontent.com/pod-product-compliance
Lightning Source LLC
Chambersburg PA
CBHW071227170626
46809CB00005BA/1973